The Dogon

Written by **Joanne White**

Illustrated by **James Cottell**

Dedications;
For Darren, Christian and Josh, my everything
…And for all the Dogons and Griffcats still waiting for a good home!

A million thanks to:

James Cottell, for his wonderful illustrations
that have brought this story to life.

Viv and Dave, for being all round generous, selfless people
who take care of our very own rescue dog like one of their own.

My family, Mr Gamble and Miss Clegg, for supporting and believing in me.

- Joanne

Dear Reader,

Thank you for choosing this book!
I really hope you enjoy it.
If you do, it would be great to hear about it so
please consider liking
The Dogon's facebook page, @thedogonbook,
or leave a review on Amazon or Good Reads.

Now to the story………!

Best wishes,
Joanne

The first time they set eyes on him,
they knew this was the one;
a real handsome fella,
as friendly as they come.

He pleaded with his big brown eyes
and kissed them with his tongue,
"please take me home with you today,
to you I do belong!"

A week later they collected him
and then they took him home,
with no idea how rare he was,
his origins unknown.

For this was no ordinary dog, oh no,
this was a Dogon;
a cross between a dog (of course)
and a fire breathing dragon!

By day he is a normal dog,
snoozing in the afternoon..

... by night he is a dragon
by the light of the full moon.

The first time that they realised,
they'd let him out to do his business;
little did they know
just what it was they were to witness!

He flew up into the air,
so majestic and so free!
It's not what they'd expected,
they'd only let him out to pee!

They gasped in astonishment
and wondered if he would return;
he came back before sunrise,
a routine that they would learn.

They decided not to tell a soul,
for fear of losing him;
he could be put into a zoo,
or taken on a whim.

And so it is a secret,
the family's pet Dogon;
a cross between a dog (of course)
and a magnificent dragon!

He's proved to be quite useful,
he's great at lighting fires…..

...he's the best at toasting marshmallows
and is the most amazing flier.

Any would-be burglar
would be greeted with a fright,
should they ever try to enter
the family home at night!

A one of a kind guard dog,
the family's pet Dogon;
a cross between a dog (of course)
and a terrifying dragon!

The family often wondered about his history;
Could it be that there were more like him?
It was quite the mystery

Perhaps, one day, they will find out
—I'll be sure to let you know.
In the meantime, keep a watchful eye
upon the full moon's next show…

…..You may have yourself a Dogon,
or a Griffcat too!
There could be others out there
and they might belong to YOU!!!!